Contents

A Letter from Julia Donaldson

When I was little, my sister and I were always creating imaginary characters and putting on shows. And when I was a teenager I wanted to be an actress. Instead I became an author and wrote lots of books, but I've always loved the theatre, and writing and acting in plays too. During my two years as the Children's Laureate I created a website, www.picturebookplays.co.uk, to help children, parents and teachers enjoy acting out stories.

I often go on school visits and put on events at festivals and theatres. I like to invite children up onto the stage to take part in the show, and this gave me the idea of creating a play version of my story, *What the Ladybird Heard*, that a whole class could act out together. I hope you enjoy turning your stage, classroom, or even your living room at home, into a farmyard!

Julia Donaldson

The What the Ladybird Heard Play

The Characters

This part could be shared, or read by a teacher.

Narrator

Cow

Hen

Horse

Hog

Goose

Duck

Sheep

Dog

Cat 1

Cat 2

Ladybird

Farmer

Hefty Hugh

Lanky Len

Policeman 1

Policeman 2

All animals

*Animals take up their places in the farmyard,
herded in by the farmer.*

Once upon a farm lived a fat red hen,
A duck in a pond and a goose in a pen,
A woolly sheep, a hairy hog,
A handsome horse and a dainty dog,
A cat that miaowed and a cat that purred,
A fine prize cow...
And a ladybird.

 And the cow said

 MOO!

 and the hen said

 CLUCK!

 HISS!

 said the goose and

 QUACK!

 said the duck.

 NEIGH!

 said the horse.

 OINK!

said the hog.

 BAA!

 said the sheep.

 WOOF!

 said the dog.
One cat miaowed

 MIAOW!

 while the other one purred,

PRRRRRRR!

And the ladybird said never a word.
But the ladybird saw,
And the ladybird heard ...

STAGE LIGHTS DIM

Enter Hefty Hugh and Lanky Len. They mime driving a van, then stop and look at a map. One of them holds a big key (the key to the cow's shed).

 She saw two men in a big black van,
With a map and a key and a cunning plan.
And she heard them whisper,

 This is how
We're going to steal the fine prize cow:

 Open the gate at dead of night.

 Pass the horse and then turn right.

 Round the duck pond, past the hog.

 Be careful not to wake the dog.

 Left past the sheep,

 Then straight ahead

 And in through the door of the prize cow's shed!

Hugh and Len mime driving away.

STAGE LIGHTS UP

And the little spotty ladybird
(Who never before had said a word)
Told the animals,

This is how
Two thieves are planning to steal the cow:
They'll open the gate at dead of night.
Pass the horse and then turn right.
Round the duck pond, past the hog
(Being careful not to wake the dog).
Left past the sheep, then straight ahead
And in through the door of the prize cow's shed!

And the cow said

 MOO!

 and the hen said

 CLUCK!

 HISS!

 said the goose and

 QUACK!

 said the duck.

 NEIGH!

 said the horse.

OINK!

 said the hog.

 BAA!

 said the sheep.

 WOOF!

 said the dog.

 And both the cats began to miaow:

 MIAOW!

 We *can't* let them steal the fine prize cow!

 But the ladybird had a good idea
And she whispered it into each animal ear.

The ladybird whispers to all the animals.

At dead of night . . .

BLACKOUT
Enter Hugh and Len, on foot, creeping.
They have the map and key, and a torch.

 the two bad men
(Hefty Hugh and Lanky Len)
Opened the gate while the farmer slept
And *tiptoe* into the farm they crept.

During the following section, Hugh and Len tiptoe round
the stage, following the trickster noises and so going
in the wrong direction.

 Then the goose said

 NEIGH!

 with all her might.
And Len said,

 That's the horse – turn right.

 The dainty dog began to

 QUACK!

 The duck!

 We must be right on track!

  OINK!

 said the cats.

 There goes the hog!

 Be careful not to wake the dog.

BAA BAA BAA!

 said the fat red hen.

 The sheep! We're nearly there now, Len.

 Then the duck on the pond said

 MOO MOO MOO!

 Just two more steps to go now, Hugh!

And they both stepped into the duck pond – SPLOSH!

Hugh and Len mime falling into the duck pond.
STAGE LIGHTS COME HALF UP
Enter Farmer, with phone.

 And the farmer woke and said

 Golly gosh!

 And he called the cops, and they came –

Enter two policemen, miming driving a car.

 NEE NAH!

 And they threw the thieves in their panda car.

The police mime bundling Hugh and Len into the
back of their car and driving off.

Then the cow said

 MOO!

 and the hen said

 CLUCK!

 HISS!

 said the goose and

 QUACK!

 said the duck.

 NEIGH!

 said the horse.

 OINK!

 said the hog.

BAA!

 said the sheep.

 WOOF!

 said the dog.
And the farmer cheered

 Hooray!

 and both cats purred,

  PRRRRRRR!

 But the ladybird said never a word.

Bringing the Play to Life

The What the Ladybird Heard Play can be performed on a real stage, in your classroom, or at home in your living room.

The Play for Large Groups

If you're putting on this play with your class, you might need some extra parts so everyone can have a role. You could have more than one narrator and take turns. Or you could have groups of some animals and change the text slightly, for example, 'some geese in a pen' instead of 'a goose in a pen'. You could also have a group of hogs, sheep and dogs. It would be harder to have groups of the other animals as this would spoil the rhyming. For instance, 'ducks' doesn't rhyme with 'cluck'!

Lighting

If the play is performed on a stage that has lighting, then it works well to dim the lights for Len and Hugh's first scene and to have a blackout for their second appearance, when they use their torch. If you're performing the play at home or in a classroom, just turn off the lights for the blackout on page 17, then turn them back on when you get to page 22. Being in charge of lighting is an important job. If you're not keen on having a speaking part, perhaps you could take the role of lighting director.

Stage Positions

When Len and Hugh are tricked, the animals should try to stand in the right place so that when they start making the wrong noises, everyone sees the robbers going off in the wrong direction. You could have a look at the farmyard picture on the contents page as a guide to where the animals might be positioned. Or, if that seems a bit complicated, it works well for the characters to line up on the stage when Len and Hugh come to steal the cow, and then make the wrong noises as the robbers go towards them.

Getting into Character

Think about how each animal moves – do they get around on two legs, or four? Do they have wings? Do they move fast or slowly? It's important to really get into your animal character so it's even funnier when you start making the noise of a different animal.

Props

Have a look around to see if you have any of the following that might be used as props: a torch, a map, a key, a phone, two police hats, beanie hats for Len and Hugh, some blue material for the duck pond and a hat or a smock for the farmer (maybe you could borrow a shirt from an adult – you just need to put it on backwards and it becomes a smock).

How to Make a
Ladybird Finger Puppet

The star of the show is the little ladybird, who should be on the stage at all times, even though she isn't always the centre of attention. The person playing the ladybird could fly this finger puppet throughout the show.

You will need:

- Black, red and white craft foam or felt
- Some PVA glue
- Safety scissors

1. Cut a black circle (approx 10cm across) out of the black foam, then cut it in half so you have two matching semicircles. These will make up the ladybird's body.

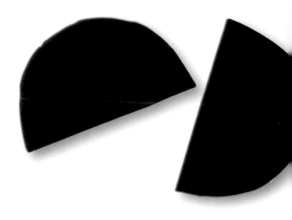

2. Cut a slightly smaller circle out of the red foam for the ladybird's wings, then cut out four little black circles for the ladybird's spots.

3. Cut the red circle in half, then stick two black spots on each wing with the PVA glue.

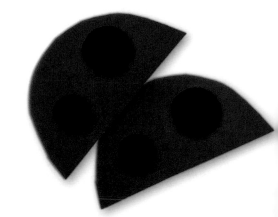

4. Now it's time to give the ladybird some antennae and her six legs. Cut eight thin strips of black foam. Take one of your black semicircles, then dab glue all around the curved edge and most of the bottom, but make sure you leave a glue-free space in the middle for your finger! Then stick on the strips for the antennae and the legs.

5. Stick the other black semicircle on top, pressing down so the two semicircles stick together, sandwiching the legs and antennae in between. Then cut out two very small white circles and two even tinier black ones. Stick the black circle on the white circle, then the white circle onto the ladybird's body for her eyes.

6. Then all you need to do is stick the wings on. Stick one on the front and one on the back, with the dots all facing the same way. Your ladybird is ready to fly away!

TOP TIP
If you want your ladybird to look the same on both sides, just turn her over and add eyes and spots to the other side.

Puppet Play
You could try making finger puppets for all the characters, and perform the play as a puppet show.

Activities

Make a Map for Len and Hugh

When the two robbers are plotting their crime, they have a hand-drawn map. Perhaps you could make one similar that could be used as a prop during the play. Have a look at this one and see if you can copy it.

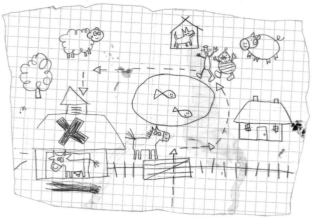

Make a Ladybird Trail

In the original picture book, the little ladybird leaves a glittering trail wherever she goes. Maybe you could create a trail for your audience, which leads them to where the play is being staged? Cover a big sheet of paper or card in glitter and leave it to dry. Then cut it up into smaller strips and place them in a trail to the stage. They could go along the floor, or maybe you could blu-tack them to a wall. Try not to make them too small though — remember you'll have to clear them up afterwards!

Advertising

Posters are a great way to let people know when and where the play is happening, and you could also design tickets for your audience with someone in charge of checking them when people arrive. You could also make a programme that tells everyone who the actors and other helpers are. This is a great souvenir for your audience.

Masks

You could make masks for your animal characters. On the next two pages there is a simple mask shape for each animal. Perhaps you could copy the mask shape of the animal you are playing onto a piece of card, and then colour it in and cut it out. Make sure you draw it big enough to cover your face! You could then glue a lollipop stick to one side with some PVA glue so you can hold it up, or add ribbon ties. Or maybe you could ask an adult to photocopy the next page and blow up one of the templates on a photocopier for you.

Mask Templates

Duck

Sheep

Hog

Goose

Horse

Cat 1

Cat 2

Cow

Hen

Dog

31

Quick Tips

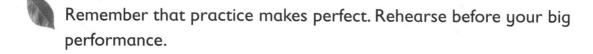

Remember that practice makes perfect. Rehearse before your big performance.

Practise your lines and ask someone to test you as you learn them.

Knowing who speaks before you and listening to what they say is called a cue. It's very important to know when you should speak, so remember to learn your cues too.

Don't forget to take a big bow at the end!

Caught the acting bug? Visit www.picturebookplays.co.uk for more play ideas.